LARGE PRINT

Animal Stories

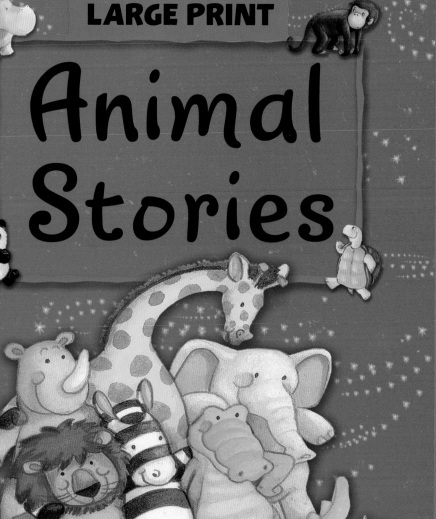

Brown Watson

ENGLAND

Monkey Mischief

The jungle animals are playing a game.
It is called Blind Jungle, and Luca Lion
is wearing a blindfold so he can't see.
He has to feel his way around and
try to guess who he finds.

Matty Monkey is bored of the game.
It is too easy! Everyone knows that
elephant has big, flappy ears, and
that giraffe has the longest neck
of any animal.

While the others play, Matty sneaks off. Look what he has found! It is the Forest Fairy's book of spells. Now Matty can have some fun. He reads one of the spells out loud.

Matty's spell changes the way his
friends all look! Luca can't even guess
which animal he has found now. It has
wrinkly skin, like Hera the elephant,
but its ears are far too small.

Matty thinks his magic has made things much more fun, but the others don't agree. They don't like being the wrong shape and size! The Forest Fairy is very cross when she founds out what he has done.

With a wave of her magic wand,
the fairy changes them all back again.
Now everyone is as they should be – except
for Matty. She has changed him into
a giant banana!

A Very Fine Family

Farrell was a small frog who lived
in the jungle. One day, he was listening
to Lamar the lion, who was boasting about
his relatives. He told everyone how
great and brave they all were.

Farrell spoke to his mum about Lamar. "Take no notice!" she smiled. "I have brought up hundreds of your brothers and sisters, and they are just as good as Lamar's relatives."

"Each baby frog starts life as a tiny tadpole. No one knows what kind of frog they will be when they grow up. Who would have thought your little sister would win a gold medal at long jump?"

"Who could have imagined that your brothers would be so good at singing? All I can do is care for each and every one of you, and see what you will become."

Farrell started to think about his family in
a different way. "Of course!" he said.
"Big brother Franco fought in the war...and
the triplets are famous ballerinas now.
But what about me, Mum?"

His mum gave him a big cuddle.
"Just look at your homework,
Farrell," she smiled. "Five out of
five every time, and a big star.
You're the brains of the family!"

The Right Rewards

Ringo Rabbit lives in the countryside, near a wood. He used to love his home, but recently it has become very messy. People bring their picnics, but leave their rubbish behind when they go.

Poor Ringo tries to keep the place
tidy, but there is just too much mess.
He decides to ask his friends,
Bertie and Gertie Fieldmouse,
for their help.

Bertie and Gertie know what it is like to live near humans. They live on a farm, with lots of lovely corn to eat. Their human, the farmer, is much more kind to the countryside than many others.

Together, the animals scamper back
to tidy up the forest. On the way, they
find Hazel, the squirrel. She is sad.
The rubbish is so stinky that she can't
smell where she has hidden half
of her nuts!

Gradually, more and more
animals come along to help with the
woodland tidy up. As they throw away
all the old food, bits of paper and
crumpled wrappers, a fairy appears.

"Well done, all of you! You really do care for your forest. As a reward for your hard work, you shall have a picnic feast of your own. Just remember to tidy up afterwards!"

A Birthday Surprise

It is Kaylee Koala's birthday and she is very excited. She can't wait to celebrate. But nobody has been to see her! What she doesn't know is that the animals are planning a surprise party for her.

Old Tortoise has written the names of all of Kaylee's friends. He asks Mister Mole to visit each of the names on the list, and invite them to the party. "Don't forget – it's a surprise!" he says.

Soon, all of the animals are talking about Kaylee's birthday party. "What present shall we give her?" wonder Susie Snake and Freddie Frog. "Do you think she would like some grubs to eat?"

Koalas don't eat grubs, so that's no good.
"I've brought some fish for Kaylee!" says
Pinga, the pelican. But koalas don't eat
fish, either! They only eat eucalyptus
leaves. The animals think harder.

Kendra Kangaroo has the perfect present for Kaylee. She is her best friend, after all! She gives her some drawing things, for Kaylee is good at art. "Thank you so much!" smiles Kaylee.

Then all of her friends jump out of the bushes. "Surprise!" they shout. "Happy birthday!" Kaylee has such a lovely time, with lots of presents, balloons and dancing.

Later on, when all of her friends have gone home, Kaylee tries to find her drawing things. Her mum is very cross. "How can you have lost your lovely present so soon?"

Kaylee is sad, until Kendra comes back to see her. "You silly koala!" she says. "Don't you remember? You put your presents in your pouch to keep them safe during the party. There they are!" Now Kaylee's birthday is happy once more.

A Real Star

Layla the starfish was unhappy. Everyone she knew was being made miserable by Diego the shark. He was such a bully. He loved to scare all the creatures in the sea, even the other sharks.

Diego thought it was a great joke to snap his mighty jaws and frighten everyone with his rows of sharp teeth. He also had fun chasing the others, and making them crash into the rocky seabed.

There wasn't a single creature in the ocean that wasn't afraid of Diego. But Layla figured that if they all worked together, they might be brave enough to face him and teach him a lesson.

Some of Layla's fishy friends started
the plan. They played and laughed
where Diego could hear them. He was
sure to come and try to spoil their fun.

Sure enough, Diego heard them enjoying themselves, and decided to swim by. He would soon make them feel miserable – and that would be great fun for him. "Ready or not, here I come!" he thought.

Layla gave the signal. "Diego is coming!" whispered Cindy Squid to Vito the Lobster. "Be brave – I'm here with you!" And 1–2–3…Vito clamped down his claws as hard as he could on Diego's nose.

Diego cried out in surprise and swam
off looking very embarrassed. The
other creatures saw him speeding
away to hide behind some seaweed.
"Hurray!" they sang. "We did it!"

The creatures all cheered for Layla. She was the one who realised they had to stand up and be brave. "You are a star!" they cried. "And you shine brighter for us than anything in the night sky. We love you, Layla!"

A Lesson for Maria

Maria is a naughty mouse. She makes up stories all of the time. The other day, she pretended she was ill so that she didn't have to go to school.

"Oh, Mummy, I'm so hot and itchy
and spotty!" she said. Mummy Mouse
tucked Maria into bed and gave her
lots of magazines. She even let her
watch TV and eat ice cream.

Naughty Maria gave away her secret when she went swimming in the river. Mummy and Nanny Mouse found her, and saw that her spots weren't real. They were SO cross. But Maria didn't learn.

Maria's next fib was to her friends. She told them that the house by the forest was haunted. "Really, it is!" she insisted. "But I'm not scared. I'll even go inside."

Maria's friends all believed her. They thought she was very brave. She wasn't though. Her cousins and auntie lived in the house and there weren't any ghosts.

When her cousins heard what she had done, they were shocked. "Maria!" they gasped. "No one will believe you if you make things up all the time." Maria didn't care.

Maria asked her Mum if she could stay
at the twins' house for a sleepover.
"Well you can…" said Mummy Mouse,
"but we're going to the seaside so you'll
miss out." Maria didn't believe her.

Maria was sure that her mum was playing a trick. She went to stay with the twins. Imagine her surprise when she got home to find that her family had been to the beach after all. Not everyone makes things up, Maria!

Home Sweet Home

The Henderson family are very busy. Their hen house needs a coat of paint to make it look fresh and new. "Look, look! It's such a lovely home!" they cluck.

Bess and Billy Bunny
have a lovely home as well.
It is warm and dry and full of straw.
The door shuts tightly to keep
out anything scary at night.

"We're so lucky," snuffles Billy Bunny. "Richie tidies up for us every day and brings us fresh food. And every week we get fresh straw to lie on." Bess twitches her nose and agrees with him.

Cilla the ginger cat is happy, too. Her owner lets her sleep indoors. She has a cosy basket with blankets, and toys to play with. "It's just purrrrfect," she tells her friends.

Cilla the cat needs her home to be warm and safe right now, for she has just had babies! She has eight cute kittens to look after. They love to snuggle up close and fall asleep in their basket.

"RRRRuff!" barks Zeus. "But none of you gets a bath from your master like I do!" He loves feeling the warm water and bubbles in his fur. It isn't so nice when he gets soap in his eyes, though.

Scruff doesn't agree at all.
"Who wants to be clean?" he woofs.
"Dogs are made for digging! And
that means getting dirty!" Being in
the mud makes Scruff very happy.

Molly the little snail hears all of this and looks at her mum. Her mum just smiles. "I'm glad they're all so happy," she says. "But what a fuss! They should just carry their home with them, like us!"

Lions Don't Lie

Little Zachary Zebra is all alone today. He wanders through the trees, wondering if he will find someone to play with. Then he hears a noise. WAAH! A scary crocodile makes him jump.

Zachary is still shaking when he hears a thundering noise. What can THAT be? Phew – it's just Halla the elephant. She sees that Zachary looks scared and says, "Come on, stick with me."

Halla takes Zachary to find Kosey Lion.
He looks bored. "What are you doing today,
Kosey?" they ask. "Hmm, nothing much,"
he says. "Maybe I'll go to the shops."

"Really?" they ask. It seems unlikely. Then Kosey roars with laughter. "No, not really! Actually, I'm going to visit my Uncle Ochi in hospital." Zachary and Halla look at each other.

"Really?" they ask. It seems unlikely. Then Kosey laughs again. "No, not really! Actually, there's a three-legged race over near the river. Do you want to come?" Zachary and Halla look dubious.

"Really?" they ask. It seems unlikely. Then Kosey laughs again. "No, not really! Actually, I have to get my mane cut by the hairdresser." Zachary is confused. Toucan says he'll follow Kosey to find out the truth.

"You won't believe this!" squawks Toucan. "Kosey really has gone for a haircut!" The other animals rush to the hairdresser. Sure enough, Kosey is waiting for a trim.

When his mane is tidy, Kosey grins at his friends. "So, you guys," he says. "This afternoon I'm going to go motorcycle racing – do you want to come?" The others all laugh. Kosey just loves to make things up!

Animal Explorers

Miss Newman is teaching her class about animals around the world. "Does anyone know an animal that lives in Australia?" she asks. Joe puts up his hand.

"Sharks, Miss! Big, scary ones with hundreds of teeth!" Miss Newman laughs. "You're right, Joe. Great white sharks live in the seas around Australia – and some other, less scary sharks, too!"

Cassie has an idea. "Do platypuses live in Australia? I saw one in the zoo and it was reeeeeally weird looking." Miss Newman nods her head. "They are one of the most unusual creatures on the planet."

Miss Newman points to the Antarctic. "What creatures live here?" Charlie shouts out, "Lions!" and everyone laughs. Then he says penguins, which is much more sensible.

Each of the children is given a picture and must try to find where their animal lives. Annie has a parrot, and knows that they live in the rainforest.

"What about unicorns, Miss? Where do they live?" asks Betty. Her teacher explains that they only live in stories, not in a real country of the world. Betty looks a bit sad.

Now the children have some real fun.
Miss Newman asks them to paint a
picture of their favourite animal.
"You can even paint a unicorn, if
you like," she whispers to Betty.

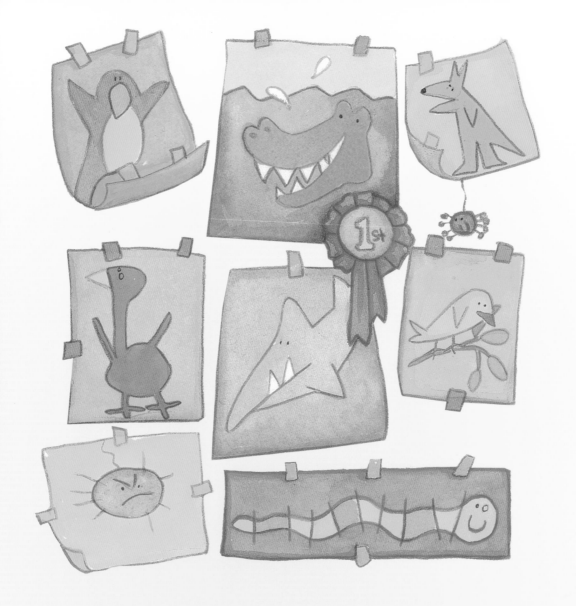

The children concentrate so hard they hardly notice when it is break time. Their finished pictures are amazing. Miss Newman decides to stick them on the wall for people to admire. Well done, everyone!

The Magic Wishing Tree

Keira's house was near a wood. She loved to look out of her bedroom window and imagine what was happening with all the creatures that lived there.

Sometimes Keira's dad took her walking in the wood to see what they could find. "Look at the squirrels, Dad!" She saw birds, too, and once saw a hedgehog.

Keira never went too far into the wood, but if she had, she would have been very surprised. Right in the middle there was a very special tree. It was called the wishing tree.

This tree could make any animal's wish come true. "I wish I could find somewhere safe to sleep for the winter," said Monty Mouse. And sure enough, the tree helped him find a cosy pile of leaves, hidden away.

"I wish we had something to play,"
said the little Weasel twins. So Squirrel
kindly gave them some conkers, and
showed them how to play a game with
them. "This is FUN!" they squealed.

"I wish I could have my squeak back," said tiny Millie Mouse. And the tree made sure that Mrs Badger called round, with some of her famous cough medicine to make Millie better.

One day, Professor Owl called some of the animals together. "The tree tells me you have all been wishing you were cleverer," he hooted. "So today is going to be a school day. Concentrate and you will learn many things!"

Tinchy Hedgehog had a wish,
but he wasn't sure what to do about it.
"Erm, Robin," he coughed nervously.
"How do I make a wish at the wishing
tree?" Robin cocked his head and
thought about it.

"I think if you tell me your wish, the tree will hear it," said Robin. So Tinchy told him. As soon as he spoke, the strangest thing happened. He curled into a ball and started rolling around on the ground.